YOU'VE GOT A FRIEND

WHEN YOUR FRIEND IS LONELY

BY ALLAN MOREY

EVANSTON PUBLIC LIBRARY
CHILDREN'S DEPARTMENT
1703 ORRINGTON AVENUE
EVANSTON, ILLINOIS 60201

TIPS FOR CAREGIVERS

Social and emotional learning (SEL) helps children grow their self and social awareness. They will learn how to manage their emotions and foster empathy toward others. Lessons and support in SEL help children build relationship skills, establish positive habits in communication and cooperation, and make better decisions. By incorporating SEL in early reading, children will have the opportunity to explore different emotions, as well as learn ways to cope with theirs and those of others.

BEFORE READING

Tell the reader that feeling lonely is something everyone experiences.

Discuss: What causes you to feel lonely? How do you feel when lonely? How do you react? Do you ever notice other people reacting the same way?

AFTER READING

Talk to the reader about how to recognize when someone else is feeling alone.

Discuss: How do you talk to a friend who is lonely? What should you do and say to your friend? In what ways can you help a friend overcome his or her loneliness?

SEL GOAL

Young students struggle to understand their own emotions, and it's even more difficult for them to recognize how someone else is feeling. Being able to spot clues in a friend's body language and actions will help improve their social awareness skills. Lead a discussion about how students feel when lonely. Do they feel sad? Do they feel like no one understands them? What helps them feel better? By sharing this information with each other, students will learn how to communicate with others who might be feeling lonely.

TABLE OF CONTENTS

CHAPTER 1
Recognizing Loneliness 4

CHAPTER 2
Understanding Loneliness 8

CHAPTER 3
Responding to Loneliness 14

GOALS AND TOOLS
Grow with Goals 22
Writing Reflection 22
Glossary 23
To Learn More 23
Index 24

CHAPTER 1

RECOGNIZING LONELINESS

What does loneliness look like? You might look sad and frown. You might even **pout**.

We also show this **emotion** with **body language**. We might cross our arms. We could hang our heads or **slouch**. We don't look people in the eyes.

CHAPTER 1 5

Loneliness can affect how we feel and act. It can cause us to be sad. Or we might feel **anxious**. We might not want to go out and play or talk to anyone.

ALONE TIME

Not everyone who is alone feels lonely. Some people like spending time alone. They like to **entertain** themselves. They might read a book. Maybe they like to draw or make up stories.

CHAPTER 1 7

CHAPTER 2

UNDERSTANDING LONELINESS

Loneliness is the feeling of being alone. We feel lonely for different reasons. Think. What makes you feel lonely? How does it feel? That can help you understand why someone else might feel that way.

Not having anyone to play with or talk to could make your friend feel lonely. Have you ever been in this **situation**? How did it feel?

CHAPTER 2

People can feel lonely even with people near. You and your friends are at a party. Emily is feeling ignored. Everyone else is having fun. No one is **including** her. That makes her feel lonely.

CHAPTER 2 · 11

People can feel lonely when they feel out of place. Dom and his family just moved here from another country. He speaks a different language. He can't understand the others in the class. They can't understand him. He has a hard time making friends. All of this makes Dom feel anxious and alone.

CHAPTER 13

CHAPTER 3

RESPONDING TO LONELINESS

You can **comfort** someone who is feeling lonely. How? First, look for signs that the person is lonely. Is a friend or peer alone? Does he or she look sad?

Ask, "Can I sit with you?" If she is lonely, she might want someone near her. It could make her feel better. She will feel included.

CHAPTER 3

Is a friend being quiet? Ask, "Are you OK?" If he is lonely, he might want to talk. Just listen. Having someone to talk to could make him feel less alone. Tell him you are there to listen. Look at him when he talks.

HOW LONELINESS HURTS

Why is it important to stop loneliness? It can drain someone of **energy**. People who are lonely can have trouble sleeping at night. They are more likely to get sick.

Is a friend trying to talk but is being ignored? That might make him feel **misunderstood** and alone. You could help him! Ask everyone to be quiet and listen to him. Feeling heard could help him feel better.

FEELING MISUNDERSTOOD

Feeling misunderstood can make someone feel lonely. Your friend has an idea. But no one else understands it. It makes him feel lonely. Have you ever felt misunderstood? How did it make you feel?

Did you get a new neighbor? Does she live alone? You could make a card to welcome her. Or you could show her around your neighborhood. Treating her kindly keeps her from feeling lonely.

Helping others is **rewarding**. They feel better, and you will also feel good about yourself. You will have helped someone feel less lonely. You could even make new friends!

GOALS AND TOOLS

GROW WITH GOALS

Everyone gets lonely sometimes. How can you avoid being lonely and help others who may be feeling lonely?

Goal: Make a new friend! Even if someone doesn't look lonely, you can introduce yourself! Ask what that person likes. Maybe you have something in common!

Goal: Share your interests! Maybe a lonely friend is having trouble opening up. Share with him or her things that you like. This could help that person feel more comfortable talking about his or her interests.

Goal: Stand up! If you see someone alone or bullied, stand up for that person. Be there for that person so he or she isn't alone. You can help him or her overcome loneliness and other uncomfortable feelings!

WRITING REFLECTION

With a friend, write down a list of your favorite things to do.

1. Which of these things are best to do with someone else?

2. Which of these can you do by yourself?

3. Keep this list in mind. If you see someone who looks lonely, you could ask him or her to do something on the list. Or if you are alone, you could do something on the list to entertain yourself and stop yourself from feeling lonely.

GLOSSARY

anxious
Feeling worried or fearful.

body language
The gestures, movements, and mannerisms by which people communicate with others.

comfort
To calm or reassure someone.

emotion
A feeling, such as happiness, anger, or sadness.

energy
The ability or strength to do things without getting tired.

entertain
To amuse in an enjoyable way.

including
Welcoming.

misunderstood
Not understood, or not understood correctly.

pout
To push out your lips to express annoyance or disappointment.

rewarding
Offering or bringing satisfaction.

situation
The circumstances that exist at a particular time and place.

slouch
To droop or bend forward.

TO LEARN MORE

Finding more information is as easy as 1, 2, 3.

1. Go to www.factsurfer.com
2. Enter "**whenyourfriendislonely**" into the search box.
3. Choose your cover to see a list of websites.

INDEX

alone 7, 8, 12, 14, 17, 18, 21

anxious 7, 12

body language 5

comfort 14

draw 7

frown 4

ignored 11, 18

including 11, 15

language 12

listen 17, 18

misunderstood 18

moved 12

party 11

play 7, 9

pout 4

read 7

sad 4, 7, 14

sick 17

sleeping 17

slouch 5

talk 7, 9, 17, 18

welcome 21

Blue Owl Books are published by Jump!, 5357 Penn Avenue South, Minneapolis, MN 55419, www.jumplibrary.com

Copyright © 2020 Jump! International copyright reserved in all countries. No part of this book may be reproduced in any form without written permission from the publisher.

Library of Congress Cataloging-in-Publication Data

Names: Morey, Allan, author.
Title: When your friend is lonely / Allan Morey.
Description: Blue owl books. | Minneapolis: Jump!, Inc., [2020]
Series: You've got a friend | Includes index. | Audience: Ages 7–10. | Audience: Grades 2–3.
Identifiers: LCCN 2019039840 (print)
LCCN 2019039841 (ebook)
ISBN 9781645272144 (hardcover)
ISBN 9781645272151 (paperback)
ISBN 9781645272168 (ebook)
Subjects: LCSH: Loneliness in children–Juvenile literature. | Loneliness–Juvenile literature.
Classification: LCC BF723.L64 M67 2020 (print)
LCC BF723.L64 (ebook) | DDC 152.4–dc23
LC record available at https://lccn.loc.gov/2019039840
LC ebook record available at https://lccn.loc.gov/2019039841

Editor: Susanne Bushman
Designer: Molly Ballanger

Photo Credits: annebaek/iStock, cover; Alfa Photostudio/Shutterstock, 1; Sebastian Enache/Shutterstock, 3; Dean Drobot/Shutterstock, 4; Rozochka/Shutterstock, 5; MoMorad/iStock, 6–7; sunabesyou/Shutterstock, 8; Zurijeta/Shutterstock, 9; SolStock/iStock, 10–11 (background); Luis Molinero/Shutterstock, 10–11 (foreground); fstop123/iStock, 12–13, 16–17; PeopleImages/iStock, 14; New Africa/Shutterstock, 15; monkeybusinessimages/iStock, 18–19, 20–21.

Printed in the United States of America at Corporate Graphics in North Mankato, Minnesota.